THIS CANDLEWICK BOOK BELONGS TO:

_____

_____

_____

_____

To Joe
S. M.

For Rachel
I. B.

Text copyright © 1996 by Sam McBratney
Illustrations copyright © 1996 by Ivan Bates

All rights reserved.

First U.S. edition 1997

Library of Congress Cataloging-in-Publication Data

McBratney, Sam.
Just one! / Sam McBratney ; illustrated by Ivan Bates.—1st U.S. ed.
Summary: Digger the squirrel wonders how to carry home the big pile of blackberries that he and his
friend have picked, but the problem is solved when various animals come to sample the berries.
ISBN 0-7636-0223-X
[1. Squirrels—Fiction. 2. Animals—Fiction. 3. Blackberries—Fiction.] I. Bates, Ivan, ill. II. Title.
PZ7.M478275Ju   1997
[E]—dc21   97-10175

2 4 6 8 10 9 7 5 3 1

Printed in Hong Kong

This book was typeset in Goudy.
The pictures were done in watercolor and colored pencil.

Candlewick Press
2067 Massachusetts Avenue
Cambridge, Massachusetts 02140

JUST ONE!

Sam McBratney
illustrated by Ivan Bates

CANDLEWICK PRESS
CAMBRIDGE, MASSACHUSETTS

Down in the woods, little Digger was
picking blackberries with the old gray
squirrel who looked after him.
They picked blackberries along by the
river, and they picked them
in the shady lane.
Soon they had
a big pile of
blackberries.

"Is this the biggest pile of blackberries you've ever seen?" said little Digger to Old-and-Gray.

"Yes it is," replied Old-and-Gray. "I'll go and look for something to put them in, or we'll never carry them home."

"Will I be in charge of our blackberries while you're away?" asked Digger.

"Yes. But don't eat too many— just a few," said Old-and-Gray. And off he went to find something to put the blackberries in.

A country mouse ran out of the cornfield at the edge of the woods. She sat down beside Digger and the pile of blackberries. "I'm in charge of all these," said Digger. "They look yummy," said the mouse. "Do you think I could have some?" "Well, don't eat too many," said Digger. "Just a few."

The country mouse ate some of the blackberries, and so did little Digger.

A flatfooted duck waddled up from the
river. He looked at Digger, and the
country mouse, and then he pointed
his beak at the pile of blackberries.
"Very nice indeed," said the duck.
"I'm in charge of them," said Digger.
"Do you think I could have some?"
asked the duck.
"Well, not too many,"
said Digger.
"Just a few."

The flatfooted duck ate some of the
blackberries, and so did Digger and
the country mouse.

Then a bouncy baby rabbit came out of
the woods. She hopped right around the
blackberries and sat down beside Digger,
and the duck, and the country mouse.
"Do you think I could taste some of
those yummy blackberries?" she said.
"Well, not too many,"
said Digger. "You can
just have a few."

The bouncy
baby rabbit ate some
of the blackberries, and so did Digger
and the duck and the country mouse.

Then they heard the noise of
someone approaching through the
woods. Old-and-Gray was coming back
with something to hold the blackberries.

"I hope there won't be too many to carry in this," he said as he came closer. "No," said Digger, looking at the pile of blackberries. "Not too many . . .

just one!"

Sam McBratney is the author of the enormously popular and award-winning picture book *Guess How Much I Love You,* illustrated by Anita Jeram, as well as *The Caterpillow Fight,* illustrated by Jill Barton, and *The Dark at the Top of the Stairs,* illustrated by Ivan Bates.

Ivan Bates debuted as a children's book illustrator with his art for Sam McBratney's *The Dark at the Top of the Stairs,* which *Booklist* called "appealing" and *Publishers Weekly* described as "endearing."